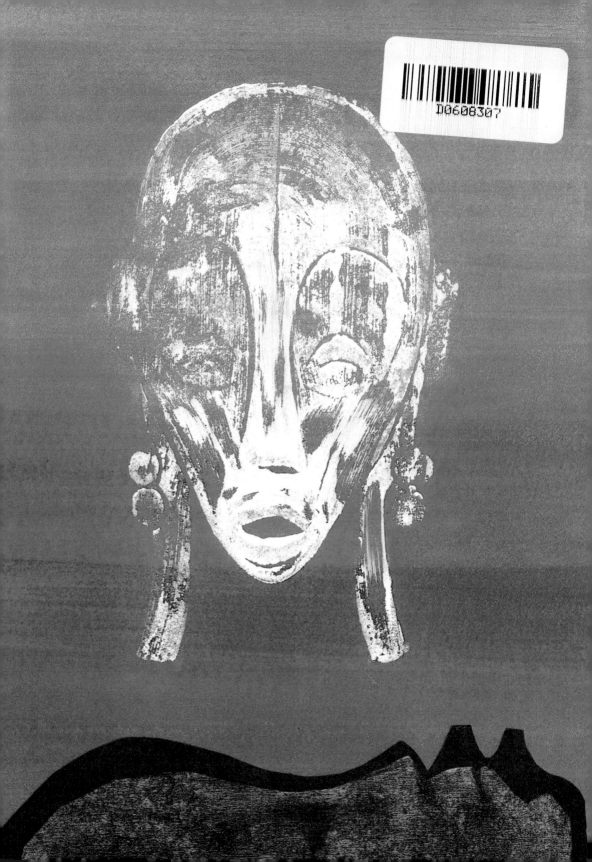

FROM THE FRENCH OF BLAISE CENDRARS

SHADOW

translated and illustrated by
MARCIA BROWN

ALADDIN BOOKS
MACMILLAN PUBLISHING COMPANY · NEW YORK
COLLIER MACMILLAN PUBLISHERS · LONDON

Aladdin Books
Macmillan Publishing Company
866 Third Avenue, New York, NY 10022
Collier Macmillan Canada, Inc.

First Aladdin Books edition 1986
Printed in the United States of America
A hardcover edition of *Shadow* is available from Charles
Scribner's Sons, Macmillan Publishing Company.

10   9   8   7   6

Library of Congress Cataloging-in-Publication Data
Cendrars, Blaise, 1887–1961.   Shadow.
"Translation of Blaise Cendrars' La Féticheuse"—
T.p. verso.
Summary: Free verse evocation of the eerie, shifting images of
Shadow which represents the beliefs and ghosts of the past and
is brought to life wherever there is light, fire, and a storyteller.
1. Shades and shadows—Juvenile poetry.
2. Children's poetry, French—Translations into
English.   3. Children's poetry, English—Translations
from French.   [1. Shadows—Poetry.   2. Africa—Poetry.
3. French poetry]   I. Brown, Marcia, ill.   II. Title.
[PQ2605.E55F4713   1986]   841'.912   86-3432
ISBN 0-689-71084-4 (pbk.)

What is Shadow?

From conversations with shamans in their villages, from storytellers around the fires in an Africa that is passing into memory, the poet Blaise Cendrars evoked a dancing image—Shadow.

Out of the fire that called forth the many images of Shadow, came the ash that was a sacred bond to the life that had gone before. The beliefs and ghosts of the past haunt the present as it stretches into the future. The eerie, shifting image of Shadow appears where there is light and fire and a storyteller to bring it to life.

—MARCIA BROWN

The eye has no shadow.
All the children of the Moon
and of the Sun,
the Earth, the Water,
the Air, the Fire,
own no shadow.
Shadow itself has no shadow.

Shadow lives in the forest.

It goes forth at night
to prowl around the fires.
It even likes to mingle
with the dancers.
Thus it is both prowler and dancer.

But it is mute.
It never speaks.
It listens.
It comes sliding right up
behind the storyteller.
Then when the last fire is out
it goes back to the forest.

But Shadow does not sleep.
It is always watching.
If you open your eyes
in your sleep,
Shadow is there.
It has already stolen back
like a thief,
and now it is spying on you.
The eye has no shadow,
but it sees Shadow
stirring the embers
until the log on the hearth
crumbles without a sound
and falls to ash.
Ash has no shadow either.
That's why Shadow is blind,
for its eyes are
two small heaps
of ash.

And so, when all the fires are out,
Shadow is blind.
It does not see a thing.
It staggers about,
arms stretched out,
trying to grab,
to hang on.
Body dragging,
it runs, it starts to fall.
Bent in two like a beggar
it reaches for a perch,
a prop.
But it does not cry out,
and calls no one.
It has no voice.

On its nightly path
it often gets bumped,
gets torn,
trips again and again,
and each time
sprawls its full length
on the ground.
But it does not cry out,
it has no voice.

Shadow is a fall.
They say also
that it is the mother
of all that crawls,
of all that squirms.
For as soon as the sun comes up,
here are the shadow people,
breaking loose, unwinding,
stretching, stirring,
branching out, teeming,
like snakes, scorpions
and worms.

That's why a person
keeps an eye on his shadow
when he wakes up,
and takes care not to step on it
when he gets up.
It could prick him
or bite him!
But Shadow says nothing.
It has no voice.

Shadow is frightening,
but there is no need to fear.
It is not death.
That's clear
because it is there every morning
and never says a thing,
while death, when it comes,
cries out. Besides,
Shadow never asks for a thing.
It has no hunger.

Even so, watch out!
For though Shadow has no voice,
like the echo,
it can cast a spell over you,
for good or bad.
It is a trickster.
It laughs behind your back.
It mocks you
and makes a fool of you.

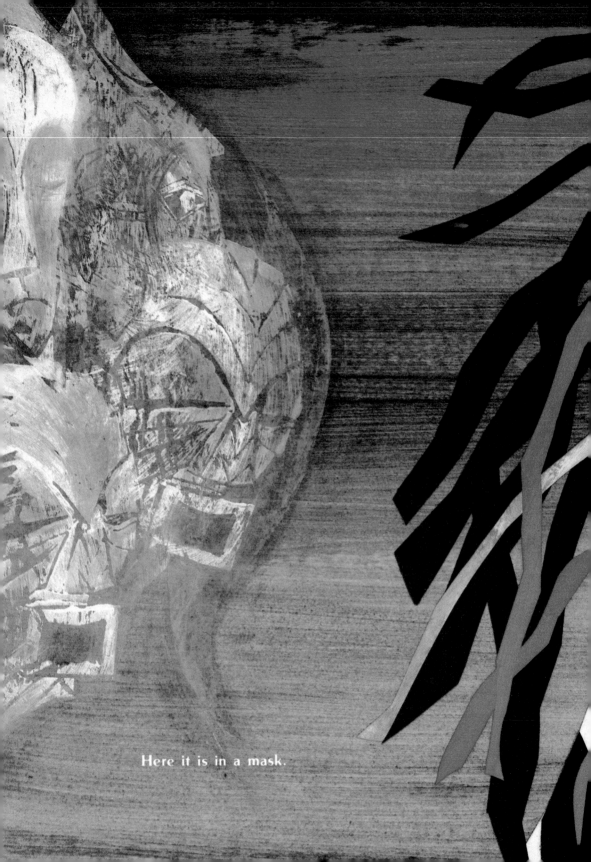

Here it is in a mask.

In the daytime
Shadow is full of life.
It waves with the grasses,
curls up at the foot of trees,
races with the animals
at their swiftest,
nestles behind the elephant's ear,
perches on a stone,
swims along with the fish.

It follows man everywhere,
even to war.

Shadow is always Shadow.
It needs no ornament,
no tattoo.
The zebra's shadow
has no stripes.

Shadow is magic.
You had better not
look at it too closely.
For is it to the left,
or the right,
before or behind,
above or below?
At noon, Shadow is everywhere.

In the evening,
Shadow spreads out;
not a hole that it does not fill,
not a hump, not a mound
that it does not double!
It even sticks to your footprints.
It lies down on the footpaths.
It chokes all the roads.
No one can pass,
for no one can push it aside,
it is so heavy.

Yes, Shadow is heavy
when night falls.

Neither the eagle
nor the vulture can raise it.
In vain they try
to soar into the air.
Their shadow flops
this way and that,
like a clumsy bat,
and crashes so heavily
to the ground, that they,
the mighty birds of the heavens,
fall after it, worn out.
No one can fight Shadow.

Go home,
build a fire.
Behold once more,
Shadow!
What is Shadow?
In the crackling coals,
is it the spark?
Light up!
The spark has no shadow.
The eye has no shadow,
but Shadow is in the eye.
It is the pupil!
Every breath stirs it to life.
It is a game.
A dance.